TALL TALES FOR TRAVELLERS

by

Michael M. Roe

AuthorHouse™
1663 Liberty Drive, Suite 200
Bloomington, IN 47403
www.authorhouse.com
Phone: 1-800-839-8640

First published by AuthorHouse 11/25/2008

ISBN: 978-1-4389-1193-9 (sc)

Printed in the United States of America
Bloomington, Indiana

This book is printed on acid-free paper.

To Lupita

Foreword

I have been prompted to write this book as in the course of my working life I have travelled a great deal, especially abroad, and, like many people, I have found it difficult to pass the time on long flights.

The in-flight movies of necessity try to cater for all tastes and frequently satisfy none; the headphones are difficult to keep plugged-in and the tapes soon run out; and, it is not always possible to concentrate on work or read a serious book.

With the above in mind, *Tall tales for travellers* is intended as light reading. The eighteen stories are short, consequently it is hoped that the reader will find it easy to pick up and put down either to snooze or escape having to talk to your neighbour.

All the stories relate to unusual experiences and happenings and many are travel related.

If the stories help make a long journey pass more agreeably and bring a smile, I will have achieved my aim.

Bon voyage!

Michael M. Roe

(mmroe@hotmail.com)

August 2008

*"One's destination is never a place, but
a new way of seeing things"*
— Henry Miller —

*"The world is a book and those who do
not travel read only one page"*
— St. Augustine —

Contents

It is more than my job is worth

I was nineteen and had just completed my first year at university. I was enjoying the experience but found the conflict of having few responsibilities and the need to study somewhat difficult. I needed to come to terms with a new discipline without the enforced conformity of a boarding school environment. I accepted this but it left a vacuum. I had to learn to stand on my own two feet. The idea was daunting in spite of having my full share of adolescent cockiness.

The long summer vacation was in front of me; I was without financial resources and could only dream of lounging on a sunny beach with a bikini clad beauty, unlike some of my fellow students who were planning to act the playboy in their father's Riviera holiday home.

Initially, I dwelt on how unfair life can be but realized that I had to come to terms with financial needs. I was going to have to get a summer job.

Colleagues in similar circumstances and with previous experience informed me where to look for work. I learnt, for example, that they had worked as holiday camp helpers, bus conductors, construction workers, waiters, office clerks and shop assistants. I resolved to follow their lead.

The problem was to know how to go about applying. The smarter students, or those who had had previous experience, knew that the more attractive and better paying jobs had to be secured well in advance. Being unfamiliar with the process, I was starting late and had missed out on the more attractive possibilities.

Apparently, the secret involved contacting the major retail, catering, tourist, construction and transport companies during the Easter period when these companies were assessing their staffing needs for the coming summer season. I had obviously missed out on the best opportunities, but given my need, I started telephoning the personnel departments of some of these companies.

In my naivety, I asked each time to speak to the Personnel Manager only to be cut short by the secretary and referred to a junior clerk. I was invariably summarily rejected. My first contact with the real world was proving less than auspicious. My financial needs, however, were more important than my sensibilities and so I persevered.

Finally, after trying yet again to speak directly to the Personnel Manager of a large retail group, I was referred by his secretary to a female subordinate who, it seemed, instinctively sensed my desperation and showed sympathy for my plight. She informed me that the summer jobs favoured by most students had long been taken but that there was an emergency need in the Bedding Department of one of their major department stores resulting from the unexpected absence of a delivery boy.

—Would I be interested?

—Of course.

The job was explained in the following way:-The Bedding Department was a special case due to the weight and size of the items and required the use of specially adapted vehicles. The job also required an early start as the beds took time to load and deliveries were made over a wide geographical area.

— Was I still interested?

—Of course.

—Was I fit and strong enough to work as a delivery boy?

—Of course.

—If you are still interested you need to come for interview this afternoon and be prepared to start the next day. Would this be acceptable?

—Of course.

I dressed up in my grubbiest jeans so as to look the part and hastened to the Personnel Department. After a friendly chat with the Personnel Assistant over "a nice cup of tea", I was duly given the job. The wage would just about pay for my temporary lodgings and food, but at this point I did not care.

The next morning I found my way to the store and to the Transport Depot at the back of the building. I presented myself to the Dispatch Manager and learnt that Bill, my new boss, had not yet arrived. It was suggested that I go to the Staff Canteen and have breakfast. I was hungry but broke and had to satisfy my hunger with a piece of buttered toast and a mug of sweet tea. But the bacon smelt delicious.

At 7.30 I returned to the Transport Depot, Bill was just arriving. He must have been about fifty, thin and wiry with a prematurely wrinkled expression. This was no doubt due to the physical demands of his job which he had been doing since his mid twenties. Although I thought that I had dressed the part in my old jeans and a sweatshirt his welcoming remark was that he supposed that I was another of these "know all" students. I smiled and mumbled a greeting.

I stood at the open area of the depot while Bill disappeared to collect the dispatch orders and delivery instructions. He returned clutching a clipboard and we then proceeded to load a number of beds, headboards and mattresses and prepared for our first delivery. For a moment he seemed less dour and appeared to smile. I was soon to discover why.

Bill was a man of few words but we established a reasonable relationship. I learnt that after doing his military service in the Far East, he had joined the store as a warehouse stockman and had been promoted to delivery driver. He had been delivering beds for nearly twenty-five years and there was nothing he did not know about delivering, including all the tricks and shortcuts.

The first delivery was to a smart address not far from the store. Bill explained that there was no point in arriving before 9.30 as to call earlier frequently embarrassed the lady of the house who in all likelihood would have probably only just seen her husband off to work and would now be enjoying a cup of coffee in her dressing-gown. It was still only 8.30 and he decided it was time for a break. We went to a nearby café where it was apparent that he was well-known. We sat down with a hot drink and read the newspapers for an hour before we set off for the first delivery.

On arrival at our first destination, we were met by an overbearingly polite and condescending lady and Bill winked at me which, I imagined, meant that I was to follow him and keep mum. The house was a tall building with lots of stairs and we struggled with the bed to the top floor trying on the way up to avoid the oil paintings and the chandeliers. On reaching the top floor, the lady explained that the room used to belong to her daughter but she had recently got married and now lived down the road. The need for the new bed was to convert the room into an additional guest room. We acknowledged our understanding with feigned interest.

Once the bed was in place, we were perspiring as a result of our efforts but also at relief that we had not damaged anything on the way up. We were thanked profusely in a gushing and patronizing way and we pretended to be grateful for her appreciation.

As we descended the stairs, she asked Bill if he would oblige by delivering the bed that was being replaced to her daughter who lived nearby. Bill with exaggerated humility explained that to do this would be against company regulations however much he might wish to please such a fine lady as herself, and added it would be more than his job was worth. On completion of this well rehearsed speech, he continued down the stairs without saying another word. As we reached the front door, the lady grabbed her handbag with a flourish and said:

—My good man, I will make it worth your while.

Whereupon she handed him the equivalent of a day's wage.

Bill grabbed the cash and, as meekly as he could manage, mumbled he was a poor and humble man and a little extra would be a great help. We climbed into our vehicle smartly and set off for the daughter's house.

As we completed the delivery to the daughter's house and were about to leave she asked Bill if he could dispose of the bed being displaced. Bill gave his speech about company regulations and again, with exaggerated humility, explained that it would be more than his job was worth. However, for a fine young lady such as herself, unused to disposing of unwanted second hand furniture, he would like to help but she must understand it would be a special favour. Flattered by his deference, she opened her handbag and like her mother gave him the equivalent of a day's wage. I was flabbergasted. Bill was indeed the master of his trade.

When we were back in the vehicle, I complimented Bill on his skills to which he replied that we were not done yet. As we set off, instead of checking the address and details of the next delivery, he headed in the direction of a well-known flea market. He explained that we were now going to sell the bed and I then realized how new I was to the ways of the world.

Bill went straight to the second hand furniture shop of a friend and I heard him explain that he had another bed to offer him, emphasizing that it had come from a good home. Without even bothering to examine the bed, the friend handed him a wad of notes and thanked him. It was apparent that this was not the first occasion that this type of exchange had taken place between them. We then offloaded the bed and climbed back into the lorry.

By now it was only twelve o'clock and Bill suggested we finish for the day and go and have a celebratory lunch. When I naively enquired about the remaining deliveries, he explained that was not a problem as when we returned to the depot he would submit a report explaining that there was nobody at home to take the deliveries.

I was aghast at the deviousness, but willingly accepted his generous offer of half the takings. We enjoyed a drunken lunch and I went back to my lodgings looking forward to the next day and, of course, to the now affordable bacon sandwich.

An unfortunate mistake

Fuelled by the media, the Middle East is perceived as a land of oilfields, nomadic tribes, religious extremists and terrorists. This immediate response to the mention of the Middle East is rarely questioned other than by those who have spent time in the area.

It is of course undeniable that there are major conflicts in certain parts of the Middle East whose resolutions would make the world a happier place, but coverage of these developments hogs the media to the exclusion of almost all other considerations. It is rare that the media covers Arab achievements in the arts, business and sport, or refers to a culture that includes, *inter alia*, the world's oldest universities, renown scholars and Nobel Prize winners. Many of the people are educated, cultured and peace loving whose Muslim faith is about loyalty, respect, hospitality, and charity.

One of the most fascinating of modern Arab achievements is Dubai, the commercial heart of the United Arab Emirates. Until the discovery of oil in 1966, Dubai was a small village which eked out an existence fishing and pearling. It was then remote and impoverished.

Unlike many other oil rich states, the bonanza has been well managed and there has not been the political corruption, wastefulness and instability so often seen in other oil rich parts of the world. This has been the result of enlightened leadership by the Maktoums, the ruling family, and the close working relationship that they have always maintained with the leading merchant families of Al-Futtaim, Al-Ghurair, Al-Habtoor and others.

From insignificance, the economy in just forty years currently exceeds that of Egypt and is second only to that of Saudi Arabia. Dubai now has one and a half million citizens, ninety percent of whom are immigrants, which in itself reflects great tolerance, and is the fastest growing city on the planet.

* * *

Mr. Majeed was a member of one of these families. From being wealthy at the time of the discovery of oil, he, like the other merchant families, has become superrich and features in Forbes annual list of billionaires.

In 1960s at the start of the great expansion, Mr. Majeed entered agency agreements with dozens of multi-national companies. Among the agency agreements was one with General Motors and within a short period of time he was importing from this agency alone huge numbers of cars, trucks, cranes and earth moving equipment. Mr. Majeed always arranged for prompt settlement through his international bankers and he was never a concern to his creditors. Nevertheless, at headquarters in Detroit there was incredulity as to how an economy the then size of Dubai was able to buy in such large quantities. It was decided to send out a representative to better understand the situation.

The representative had never travelled to the Middle East and did not know what to expect. The best hotel at the time was an adobe built building of just forty rooms with fans to counter the heat. The location of the hotel was near to the *souk* and on the edge of the creek where there was always a great deal of activity with the loading and unloading of the *dhows*. The district was noisy, smelly and uncomfortable and his disorientation was compounded by his sense of isolation as it took up to twenty four hours to book a telephone call to Detroit. He felt disconnected from the world he knew.

The day after his arrival he found Mr Majeed's office. His first surprise was how modest was the building and how ramshackle the organization of the office. He waited over an hour to meet Mr. Majeed during which time his male secretary served him glasses of sweet tea. The secretary was very courteous but his English was less than fluent. Eventually the representative was shown into Mr. Majeed's office accompanied by the secretary who acted as interpreter. The lack of English speaking staff given the international nature of the business was a further surprise.

Mr. Majeed knew only a few phrases in English but he made his visitor welcome. The representative then explained that he had some need for information but he soon realized that not only was there a communication problem but the information relating to Articles and Memorandum of Association, shareholders and directors, annual accounts, etc. did not exist.

The secretary explained that Mr. Majeed's family had been merchants for several generations; that he ran an international business; and, that he had never been asked or been expected to supply such information. He also added that in Dubai there was no statutory reporting requirement. Somewhat confused, he took his leave with the intention of seeking new instructions from superiors in Detroit.

Detroit's reaction was that the inability or unwillingness to provide standard commercial information was not acceptable. The representative reminded his superiors that this client already had dozens of agency agreements from around the world and insistence in demanding information that was non existent or considered confidential would jeopardize future dealings not only with this client but with other merchants in the area. After lengthy telephone exchanges, it was finally decided that the representative should insist on the introduction of a Western style reporting and accounting system.

The representative arranged a further meeting with Mr. Majeed and explained that, if the relationship were to be maintained, a Western reporting and accounting system would have to be introduced. Mr. Majeed recognized that Dubai would have to change if it were to open up to international business and undertook to contract a Western specialist to set up a reporting and accounting system.

* * *

Several months later, a young British chartered accountant was engaged on a two year contract. He arrived with his wife and small child and was provided with all the basic living requirements. This included a traditional Arab house enclosed in a compound with the best amenities available at the time. It was nevertheless a huge cultural shock, especially for his wife, and although the amenities included fans for cooling, a refrigerator and other household necessities, the house was in need of painting, the plumbing was poor and the electrical wiring in a parlous state. The house was also sparsely furnished and appeared not to have been lived in for a while. The cultural shock and the prospect of being in this strange environment for the next two years made them very depressed.

The wife set about making a home and with the help of a maid shopped in the local markets for food and other necessities. She tried to make the best of her situation but missed the comforts of home. There were few opportunities to meet English speaking people and she was finding it difficult to manage the baby in these circumstances.

Meanwhile, the husband went to work. The assignment was a huge task and given the unfamiliar environment, the language barrier and the lack of organizational structure, it was difficult to know where to start. He was a serious and committed professional and viewed the job as a challenge. He worked long hours and frequently came home late. This did not help his relationship with his wife who was becoming still more depressed.

He liked the job and appreciated that he was allowed to get on with it and that he was effectively his own boss. Obtaining information, establishing new reporting streams and training his two assistants were slow but he felt in time that they would be satisfactorily established and would no doubt create confidence in the group and help relations with foreign organizations. He was happy but his wife was never able to settle and she viewed the prospect of spending two years in these conditions as intolerable. She pressed her husband to return home or at least seek an increase for the extra hours that he was putting in.

He rarely had occasion to see Mr. Majeed who in effect had delegated to him complete responsibility for the new management reporting and accounting system. He went to see Mr. Majeed who greeted him cordially and appeared pleased to see him. There was a friendly exchange and after an interval he enquired as to what was the purpose of the meeting, The accountant explained that he was working long hours and that the job was proving very demanding. He asked for an increase. Mr. Majeed was sympathetic but explained that he had signed a contract and that he was not prepared to consider an increase. The accountant left and went back to work. In the evening, he explained to his wife what happened at the meeting.

A month later she pressed her husband again to go and see Mr. Majeed and if he did not agree to review the contract, she wanted to return to the UK. This ultimatum created a great dilemma. He had to decide what was more important, his marriage or his job. Reluctantly he arranged another meeting with Mr. Majeed who again welcomed him warmly but again refused to consider an increase, opening his desk draw to remind him of the signed contract.

That evening when back home, it was agreed after a heated discussion that they would secretly return to the UK.

During the course of the next two weeks, they surreptitiously purchased their air tickets and arranged for a taxi to take them to the airport on the Thursday evening, the end of the Muslim working week.

That day he returned home early and they waited the arrival of the taxi.

When this arrived they bundled everything into the car and were driven to the airport. The husband was distressed and doubted the wisdom of the decision to leave abruptly without notice but his wife was happy and appreciated that he was making the sacrifice for the sake of his family.

After paying the taxi, they gathered their luggage and unfolded the baby's push-chair in readiness to enter the terminal building and locate the check-in counter when to their amazement and embarrassment, Mr Majeed's secretary approached holding a large buff envelope. The accountant tried to put on a brave face and said to the secretary.

—Are you going away? —He enquired sheepishly.

To which the secretary replied:

—No, no. I have come to see you off. —Countered the secretary and handed the accountant the buff envelope. The accountant's hands were full but he managed to stuff the envelope into his briefcase. He then asked the secretary:

—Why are you presenting me with this and what does it contain?

To which the secretary again replied:

—Mr Majeed wanted you to have this and it contains £20,000. He also wanted you to know that he would have given you £200,000, if you had been willing to complete your contract.

At this point the accountant was feeling both elated and utterly confused. He mumbled his appreciation and regrets to which the secretary smiled. He then added:

—Please thank Mr. Majeed for his generosity, particularly in the circumstances, and express my regret that I have not being able to continue. But before I go, please tell how he knew that I was leaving.

—Well, —Replied the secretary— Mr. Majeed owns the travel agency from which you bought your tickets.

Theatre heaven

James Hurst was a graduate engineer from Manchester University and after working in the UK for three years decided that he wanted to travel. For the rest of his working life he remained overseas as a freelance engineer on large infrastructure projects such as dams, bridges, building complexes, airports and highways. Many of the assignments were in remote parts of the world and because of their size and immense costs were usually funded by aid from foreign governments and international agencies, such as the World Bank.

Like so many others who make a career of working overseas, James had become an "expat", a term which is sometimes understood derogatively but tries to make a distinction between those that emigrate and those that go overseas intending eventually to return home. In many cases, as with James, his experiences so changed him that he did not return permanently.

One of the features of working as an "expat" is that each assignment is only temporary and consequently during the course of a career, an overseas contract worker is required to relocate many times. In the first ten years, James worked in fifteen countries for periods which ranged from six months to three years. Many of these assignments were in parts of the world off the tourist map and consequently on each occasion he had had to adapt to local conditions.

When James was in his late thirties, he had of necessity learnt to become adaptable and to mix socially with people from different backgrounds. Nevertheless, his way of living was not without its drawbacks. Having to spend long periods in areas with few of the comforts of home, he had had to learn to be self-sufficient and disciplined. He read for long periods, listened to music and played cards. He also kept up-to-date with events at home and around the world through newspapers and the radio. Drinking was occasionally excessive but he was conscious of the need to avoid letting it get out of hand.

While in remote parts of the world, he missed his parents and siblings and the everyday things such as latest gossips, scandals and crazes, films and the television. He also used to dream about the pleasures of going to the local pub, participating in on-going friendships, attending sporting events and visiting bookshops.

When he was home between contracts, he always enjoyed reconnecting with his past and generally enjoyed the benefits of his accumulated savings. However, as the years went by, he felt increasingly distant from his childhood friends even to the extent that he sensed that they were bored by his experiences.

It was after the first ten years that he realized that he was now a stranger in his own country and this presented him with a dilemma. He had planned to retire early and up to this point had not given much thought to considering living anywhere else other than in the land of his birth. He had now become an observer rather than a participant in a way of life that he had previously considered his own.

* * *

On one of his contracts, he was based in the Sudan where he was working on a large irrigation project. This proved one of the least comfortable of his experiences. There was no town for miles which meant living in a construction camp. The project employed many hundreds of locals but just thirty foreign professionals.

The main relaxation was drinking and playing cards. It was during one such session that Mal, an Australian, suggested that he spend his next leave in Australia and visit his family. This appealed to him greatly as with his disillusionment about returning permanently to the UK, it would be a good opportunity to holiday somewhere other than at home.

He thanked Mal and was grateful that he would at least have contacts when he got there.

* * *

When his contract ended, James flew to Sydney and rented a service apartment for the month that he would be in Australia. For the first three weeks he toured the east coast in a rented car travelling from Melbourne in New South Wales to Brisbane in Queensland. He was fascinated by what he saw and by the people that he met. He also felt that he had gained an insight into the Australian way of life from the help that he had received from Mal's family during his various stops along the way.

He found Australia vibrant and prosperous and without the weary scepticism of the "old world". He also thought that he observed two broad cultural groups, the older generation, mainly of British descent who, much to his surprise, still clung to ways and ideas of the "old country" and the post war generations, many of whom were the descendants of immigrants from other parts of Europe with republican ideals.

James felt that he understood both points of view but was not comfortable with either. In particular, he felt that the older generation's views were outdated and out of touch with contemporary Britain.

* * *

Mal's grandmother lived in Sydney and every Sunday evening held an open house. Any member of the family was welcome to supper. The family was large and James now knew many of them from visits when driving from Melbourne to Brisbane and several of them insisted that he came to the supper, especially as it was his last Sunday before leaving Australia.

James was driven by a member of the family to a large suburban house and introduced to the grandmother who was delighted to meet someone from England. She talked at length about her English roots and how her grandfather had come out to Australia at the turn of the century. The younger members of the family had heard it all before and were smiling but James listened attentively.

In due course, they were all invited to sit down at the dining-room table and as James was the guest of honour, the grandmother insisted he sat next to her.

During the course of the meal, James was submitted to merciless ribbing by the younger generation as England had just lost yet another "test match" to the Aussies. It was of course all said in jocular fashion but it was clear that it had significance beyond just sporting prowess.

James smiled and did not respond, thereby defusing any attempt to goad him into a reaction.

Later during the meal, he engaged in lengthy conversations with the grandmother. He explained how much he had enjoyed his visit to the Sydney Opera House where he saw Joan Sutherland singing in La Traviata. He commented that he imagined that there must no doubt be an active theatre world in Australia. The grandmother seemed somewhat amused at the suggestion and began to talk at length and very authoritatively about the London theatre. He listened charmed by her enthusiasm feeling a little humbled as here was someone from the other side of the world showing greater knowledge of what was going on in London than he.

After a pause, he thought it appropriate to show interest in a topic which was obviously of importance to her. He then enquired:

—When did you last see a show in London?

—London? —She replied— I have never left Australia.

Flying solo

Mrs. Vi Bromley was eighty three and had for most of her adult life been the devoted suburban housewife. She had been married to Kenneth and had brought up two daughters, one of which was now a nurse and the other a social worker.

Vi and Kenneth were married in the 1920s. Kenneth was a very upstanding middle class gentleman who had worked all his life as a surveyor for the local municipal council. By the time he retired, the mortgage on their home had been paid and he was in receipt of a modest pension. The pension plus his life's savings meant that the family was adequately provided for.

Kenneth, like others of his generation, had endured the Great Depression and survived the Second World War in which he served as a sergeant. These early experiences had made him disciplined and cautious as well as dull.

Life was a duty and he was committed to routine and the support of his family.

Vi, by contrast, was a woman of many fantasies which had had to be suppressed to conform with her disciplined and dutiful husband. Nevertheless, the marriage was successful and reasonably happy as she had been brought up in the traditional way to accept the role of housewife and mother.

The family went on annual holidays to nearby seaside resorts and, occasionally, to foreign parts by car when the children were in their teens. Local entertainment consisted of weekly outings to the cinema and, on special occasions, the odd trip to see a show in the capital. The trips to the capital were the highlight of her life as she could indulge her fantasy of moving in higher social circles.

In her spare time, she liked to read magazines and was an avid follower of the comings and goings of the Royal Family, the so-called aristocracy and the famous. She dreamt about their lifestyle and imagined that they had much more fulfilled lives. She could not imagine that they too had their problems.

On the death of her husband in 1981, she found herself financially and emotionally liberated and with few responsibilities. Her daughters were married and had families of their own and her only near relative was a sister, ten years her junior, who had emigrated to Canada and whom she had not been seen for many years. The sister was a spinster and a retired school teacher.

Somewhat tentatively, for they had never been close and had not seen each other for years, she wrote suggesting that she make a visit to Canada. To her surprise and delight, the sister replied promptly indicating her pleasure and encouraging her to come. The sister too was, no doubt, excited at the prospect of reconnecting with her past.

When Vi's husband was alive, he always undertook the travel arrangements which he invariably made through Thomas Cook, the travel agents. Vi realized for the first time in her life that she would have to make the bookings herself. For a woman in her eighties who had led a sheltered life, this presented a challenge. Vi knew that for many years her husband had had an account with the firm and that he had always dealt with a Mr. Taylor.

Vi found it difficult to be her age and having been attractive in her youth, she had never lost her skittishness and desire to be flirtatious. These attributes gave her an exaggerated sense of confidence and she determined that she would make all the arrangements without help from her daughters, much to their concern. Now for the first time in her life, she could do things her way and she was not going to be dictated to.

Vi was aware that Mr. Taylor was a lifelong friend of her deceased husband and that he would probably take the view, like her husband, that booking arrangements were a man's responsibility. She anticipated that he would act the chivalrous gentleman and trusted family friend in an attempt to dissuade her from her travel plans. She was irritated in advance by the thought and rather than risk being dissuaded over the telephone, she decided that she would visit him in his office. This meant taking a suburban train and heading for the capital.

The undertaking required careful preparation. The day before the planned visit to Mr. Taylor, she went to the hairdressers and had her favourite 1930s suit cleaned and pressed. On the day itself, she wore a white lace blouse under the suit and court shoes which she had not had occasion to wear for over twenty years. She overdid the make-up with excessive use of rouge and painted her lips in a Greta Garbo fashion. She was not thinking of flirting with Mr. Taylor. The underlying thought was that since this was her first venture alone to the sophisticated capital, she would dress appropriately and appear as though she was accustomed to moving in well-to-do circles.

On arrival at the train terminal in the capital, she treated herself to a taxi, an extravagance which her husband would never have permitted, and was taken to the branch of Thomas Cook where Mr. Taylor worked.

At the reception desk, she asked for Mr. Taylor only to be informed that he was no longer a booking clerk but an Assistant Manager and now worked on the executive floor. The receptionist noticed she was a bit put out by the news and offered to contact him over the telephone. Vi expressed her gratitude.

Shortly afterwards, the receptionist informed her that he was coming down to meet her and in the meantime she sat in an armchair in the main hall. A few minutes later, the lift door opened and out stepped a dapper little man with greying hair and a walrus moustache wearing a carnation in his buttonhole. He strutted proudly across the hall to greet her.

—Mrs. Bromley, what a delight to meet you! I knew Kenneth for very many years and I counted him among my friends.

He then kissed her hand in an exaggerated old-fashioned manner and added:

—Please follow me and we will go to my executive office.

Vi was impressed by such gallantry.

As they came out of the lift on the executive floor, they walked along the carpeted corridor and, as Mr. Taylor approached his office, he gave instructions in a commanding voice to his secretary to bring tea and biscuits and ordered that on no account was he to be disturbed. He then ushered Vi into his office, shut the door and invited her to sit down. Vi felt privileged and imagined that this was how he received his rich and famous clients.

Mr. Taylor in seeking to do the "right thing" by his old friend and to impress Vi overdid the pleasantries. Fortunately, the exaggerated performance was lost on Vi and she was enjoying every moment.

After the pleasantries, Mr. Taylor asked what he could do for her and she explained that she had plans to visit her sister in Canada and needed his help to make the booking. As Vi had predicted, he expressed shock at such a project and gave her all the reasons that he imagined his old friend would have given. She was not in the frame of mind to be thwarted and patiently listened to his speech with no intention of agreeing.

—But Mrs. Bromley, think what Kenneth would have wished.

—Kenneth is no longer with us to object —She replied firmly.

—But Mrs. Bromley, I have been making your travel arrangements for as long as I can remember and I know for certain that you have never been on a plane or undertaken such a long journey.

She politely showed her irritation and made it quite clear that she had no intention of changing her mind.

After further exchanges, Mr. Taylor realized that it was a waste of time to try and dissuade her and reluctantly agreed to make the booking, even though he considered that he was failing his former friend and client.

After a further exchange of pleasantries which included children, bereavement, the difficulties of getting old and how times have changed, Mr. Taylor stood up indicating that the meeting was over and escorted Vi to the main entrance where he hailed her a taxi. She returned home exhausted but happy that she had achieved her objective in spite of the objections of Mr. Taylor and her daughters. She knew that in spite of his reservations Mr. Taylor was a man of his word and that in a few days she would receive the air ticket through the mail.

Apart from his pretentiousness, Mr. Taylor was a decent and caring person and, of course, very good at his job after so many years in the business. When he returned to his office and set about making Vi's travel arrangements he included a chauffeur driven car at the company's expense to take her to the airport. He also contacted a friend at the airline who worked at the airport and explained that an elderly widow of a much respected former client was travelling on a certain date to Ottawa to visit her sister. The lady had never flown on a plane and in spite of her independent spirit would need a lot of attention. His friend agreed to give her the full VIP treatment.

Three weeks later, the travel day arrived and to Vi's delight a large Mercedes with a uniformed chauffeur arrived to take her to the airport. She felt immensely important at such treatment and, as the neighbours knew of her travel plan, she was sure that they would be discreetly viewing the scene.

On arrival at the airport, the chauffeur parked outside the main terminal in an area reserved for the exclusive use of VIPs so that Vi would not have too far to walk to enter the terminal. As they went through the revolving doors they could hear over the loudspeaker:

—Would Mrs. Bromley travelling to Ottawa please may herself known to the Air Canada check-in desk?

She was reassured by the chauffeur that it was nothing to be alarmed about and he guided her to the right check-in counter. She was overwhelmed by the crowds and the hustle and bustle but, as soon as she made herself known, a uniformed porter on an electric trolley approached and indicated to her to climb aboard. This she duly did with the help of the chauffeur who then left, bidding her a safe journey.

It was now the turn of the porter to take over and he made sure that the check-in procedures were rapidly completed and then took her on the electric trolley directly to the aircraft. The trolley sped through the main hall and through behind-the-scene areas before entering onto the tarmac. She was thoroughly enjoying the attention and imagined that this was quite normal for the rich and famous.

When the trolley arrived at the foot of the steps leading to the entrance of the plane, a stewardess was waiting to help her. Once inside the plane, she saw that she was the first to board the aircraft. She was shown to a window seat and offered a fruit juice. It was explained to her that the other passengers would be arriving shortly. She sat in her seat in awe but comforted by the reassuring words of the stewardess.

Gradually, the other passengers arrived and took their seats, and when the seat next to her was occupied, she was concerned as to how she would be able to ask to visit the toilet. The occupant was a portly gentleman making preparatory arrangements to go to sleep and in the process was making it very plain, much to Vi's disappointment, that he did not want to be engaged in conversation. The stewardess returned to help with her seat-belt and after the usual pre-flight announcements, the plane taxied to the runway.

After about an hour into the flight, the stewardess came to her and asked whether she would like to visit the cockpit. She struggled out of her seat, awakening her neighbour in the process, and accompanied the stewardess to the front of the plane. She was overwhelmed at the sight of all the cockpit lights and buttons but even more by the handsome young pilot. He was of course well practiced in these types of visits and was very courteous. After a brief explanation of the control panel, he turned the conversation to topics of greater interest to an elderly lady enquiring about her family and the purpose of her trip. She was enchanted. After a suitable period, he indicated that the meeting was over and that the stewardess would guide her back to her seat. She was enjoying herself and did not want to end the conversation and, in a desperate effort to keep it going, she looked out of the cockpit window and remarked:-

—We are not going very fast.

—No, Madam, only five hundred miles an hour.

Home cooking

Jan's family came from a working class background and his father worked as a crane driver on the docks in the Port of Rotterdam. Life was hard as it was just after the war. In the 1950s, however, the government decided on a redevelopment of the docks and compulsorily purchased the surrounding land which included their home. With sufficient money to retire, Jan's parents moved away from Rotterdam and left Jan sufficient capital to start a business.

Jan was aggressive and ambitious and with the capital he bought a small boat and engaged in-land and coastal shipping. With the post war economic recovery, his business boomed and his ambition drove him to expand into to buying larger ships until after a number of years he had a fleet which then engaged in international shipping. By the 1960s he had acquired a great fortune and was well-known in Rotterdam as a successful and important businessman.

Jan had always been too busy to think of marrying but in his fifties, partly to satisfy social aspirations, he married a society widow and had a son, Pieter.

Pieter was troubled by Jan's dictatorial ways and quickly learnt to keep his distance. It was then that he became especially close to his mother as his father was always too busy to pay him much attention.

Pieter grew up spoilt by his mother with little interest in sport or hobbies preferring to spend much of his time watching television. At twenty, he had few friends, little ambition and was overweight and lazy.

The time came when Jan began to think of a successor for his business and it had always been his hope that Pieter would take over. He realized his son's shortcomings but still believed that he could make a success of him.

All Dutch children are brought up learning English, as well as German and other foreign languages, a long standing policy of the authorities in recognition of the small size of the country. Pieter spoke English but needed to acquire fluency, especially if he were to work in international business. His father, therefore, decided to send Pieter to work for a year with a shipping company in London. A further motive was the idea that separating him from his mother for an extended period might have a maturing effect and make him stand on his own feet.

Pieter had no choice but to accept his father's decision in spite of his reluctance to change his comfortable carefree existence. He was sent on one of his father's ships from Rotterdam to Harwich and from there took the train to London. He had been provided with the address of a youth hostel in the Earl's Court area of London and he found his way there on the underground.

After three days of settling in, he began his apprenticeship with the shipping company. Given his inexperience and the fact that he had just arrived in the UK his employers did not make many demands and he began to acclimatize to this new way of life. He also noted that the senior management showed him great deference knowing who his father was.

After two weeks, he decided that he could no longer tolerate the confined and restricting environment of the hostel. He decided that since his father had committed him to be in the UK for a year, he should perhaps acquire a room of his own, particularly as he was now in receipt of a salary, modest though it was. Eventually he found an affordable room in the top back of a rundown terraced house in Fulham. The room was small, only basically furnished with second hand furniture and a gas ring for cooking and heating. It was all he could afford but its attributes were that it had a television, an armchair and provided him with his own space.

He soon found that he was lonely and decided to join an English language school for foreigners. He hoped to be invited to parties and perhaps find a girlfriend in spite of his shyness. Instead, he eventually befriended a fellow Dutchman who also enjoyed pubs and pizzas. They frequently met up and would go drinking. He could not, however, afford to do this every night and so reverted to staying in and watching television.

On returning home from work one evening, he was excited to learn that Holland was playing England at football and that it was going to be televised. This interested him and he decided for once he would eat in. He went to the nearby supermarket to find something easy to prepare. He had frequently accompanied his mother to supermarkets in Holland but had never paid much attention as to what he might need to prepare a meal. Out of desperation he selected a tin of meat, a tin of peas and a six-pack.

On returning to his room he noted that there was only a short time to prepare his meal as the match was about to start. He opened the tins and emptied the contents into a saucepan, light the gas ring and waited for the contents to heat. The television was on and the match had started. He ate his meal absorbed by what he was watching. He did not pay much attention to what he was eating but vaguely registered that it confirmed his general impression about the poor reputation of English food. Without giving the matter further thought, he carried on drinking his beers and watching the match.

Later that evening having relaxed and enjoyed the beers, he got up and went to the bathroom. On his return, he noticed one of the tins protruding from the waste-paper basket which acted as a garbage can. The label read:-

"KENNOMEAT — the dog food favoured by your pet."

"Autostop"

The Catholic University of Louvain is one of the oldest universities in Europe, established in medieval times in 1425. It is located thirty kilometers east of Brussels in the Dutch speaking part of Belgium. It is an internationally known academic institution with many illustrious alumni from different parts of Europe.

In 1955 Jacques du Chaffault was twenty five and a student at the university. His home was in Brussels and as the city was only a short distance away, he frequently went home at the week-ends, doubtless with his week's washing and for some home cooking. During the week, he shared a small apartment in Louvain with a colleague.

Although the university has many foreign students from neighbouring countries, most of the undergraduates, as one might expect, are Belgium and the majority of these are from the capital. As the capital is so close, it is relatively easy for these students to return home at the week-ends but, like students from around the world, they are invariably broke and to economize resort to hitch-hiking. Given that there are literally dozens of students wanting to go home on the Friday and return on the Sunday, there is frequently congestion at the favoured hitch-hiking spots. Over the years an unwritten code has developed among the students that require them to respect the rule of "first come, first served" and not seek to jump the queue.

The main thoroughfare from Brussels to Louvain is the Route E40. At each end of this motorway, there are lights in the built-up areas. There are also barriers preventing pedestrians accessing the road. It is only after reaching the outskirts that there are no street lights and grass verges.

Louvain is well-known as a university town and many of the inhabitants are familiar with the habits of the students and are generally willing to provide a lift in spite of the fact that it is contrary to the law to stop on the highway. This situation is of course known to the local police but they turn a blind eye as long as the queues do not get out of hand.

On one cold Sunday night in January 1955 after waiting an hour, Jacques's turn finally arrived and to his delight the car that stopped was a Mercedes sport. The driver lent over the passenger's seat, lowered the window briefly and indicated that he should jump in. Jacques thanked the driver and got into the passenger's seat. He tried to see the face of the driver but in the dark all he could make out was that he was young and probably about his age.

Jacques assumed that he must be a rich fellow student who, like him, was returning to Louvain after spending the week-end with his family. They chatted about the university and the usual subject of girls and shared a few laughs. The driver was very friendly and commented that he had to behave as far as the girls were concerned as his parents had threatened to take the car away if he did not.

In a very short time the car approached the outskirts of Louvain and the street lights lit up the interior of the car. Jacques suddenly became very bashful and stammered:-

—Your Majesty! I had no idea that I was speaking with you and I apologize for being so familiar.

King Baudouin smiled and replied:

—Please, please, do not apologize, I have enjoyed your company and the conversation. It is not very often that I have the opportunity to meet somebody without all the formalities.

Royal priority

On the Atlantic side of the Caribbean there is a remote volcanic island called Valleymous. Its population has never exceeded fifteen thousand but as a result of a series of natural disasters, the economy has been devastated and the majority of the population has fled. Those that have remained number just five thousand and are mainly the elderly without the means or the connections to relocate. Those that left, in particular the younger generation, emigrated to Canada, the United States and the UK.

In spite of its remoteness, the island has had an interesting past. It became a British colony in the 1620s and, except for short periods when captured by the French, was for over three centuries a remote outpost of the former British Empire. The appeal of the location before the advent of the iron ship was as a source of wood and fresh water for the Royal Navy, these two commodities being scarce in a region consisting largely of coral islands.

In more recent times, the island's main business has variously been the export of limes, cotton, sugar cane and water to a nearby coral island. None of these activities, however, has ever been sufficient to make for a viable economy.

As the island is unlikely ever to be self-sustaining, it depends economically on grants from the British government to balance its budget. Nevertheless, in line with the move to decolonization in the 1950s and 1960s, its political status was changed from colony to that of Dependent Territory. This has allowed the island to be self-governing on domestic matters with its own parliament but ruled by the British Foreign Office on issues relating to budget, policing, foreign affairs and constitutional changes.

This constitutional arrangement is particularly resented by the local politicians who would prefer independence despite the economic risks. The Foreign Office, however, as agent for the British government, takes the moral high ground stating that it has an obligation to ensure "good governance". Both points of view are tendentious and are not conducive to good relations. The island's leaders feel humiliated and British tax payers are burdened with a never ending financial commitment without political or economic benefit.

Prior to the constitutional change, the British appointed Governor was involved in all aspects of the island's political, economic and social life but now with the constitutional change and the much reduced population, the role has become more that of a welfare officer whose principal concerns are the remaining elderly and the maintenance of contingency plans in the event of further natural disasters.

In spite of the reduced role, the post of Governor retains diplomatic status with all the pomp and circumstance befitting a representative of Her Majesty the Queen. Among the privileges are a regal official residence, resplendent with servants and palatial gardens; full colonial regalia, including the traditional white colonial uniform with plumed headgear; a uniformed chauffeur; a Landrover with right to fly the royal pennant; and, the expectation that the incumbent be addressed as "His Excellency".

These anachronisms usually bring a wry smile even to the occupants themselves who understand that these former imperial outposts have not caught up with the changed times. Intelligent men do not take these vanities seriously, but there are exceptions.

Shortly after the latest natural disaster, a new Governor was appointed. He had not been trained in the diplomatic service but had had minor consular positions during the course of a long career in the Foreign Office. It is only to be assumed that given the reduced role, the Foreign Office in its wisdom did not see the need to engage a more highly trained diplomat.

John McGlee had joined the Foreign Office straight from school at the age of eighteen in the early 1960s. During a career as a Clerical Officer, he had by dint of commitment worked his way into the Consular Service and over the years had been sent to work in the consular section of embassies in Africa and the Middle East. He was very proud of his status as a Foreign Office employee.

His appointment by the Queen as Governor of Valleymous was the pinnacle of his career and the status that it conferred with its guarantee on retirement of an OBE was the realization of a lifetime's fantasy.

On arrival at the airport in Valleymous, the new Governor was formally met by the Prime Minister and his Ministers who were waiting in line on the tarmac outside the corrugated roofed hut that acted as airport terminal. He was subsequently ushered to his waiting Landrover with royal pennant flying and driven the sixteen miles across the island to Government House, his official residence. For anyone witnessing the scene his pride was palpable.

During the settling-in period of the next few weeks, there was the formal opening of Parliament, receptions in the grounds of Government House at which he was presented to local dignitaries and the chairing of his first cabinet meeting. The local politicians, who already resented the continued influence of the ex colonial power, had difficulty taking to His Excellency as he was overbearingly patronizing and tried to assume an authority beyond his brief. He had few friends, only sycophants.

A *modus vivendi* was, however, eventually established and the routine governance of the island limped along for the duration of his two year tenure of office.

As a precaution against further volcanic eruptions, the British Government had arranged for a team of experts to monitor the volcano round the clock. It had been two years since the eruption but prior to that the volcano had been dormant for two hundred years. The experts were divided as to the likelihood of a repeat eruption so soon after the last but were recommending continuing surveillance. Any changes were to be reported to the Governor whatever the time or circumstance.

From time to time, the volcano emitted bursts of smoke accompanied by foul smelling sulphur gases.

Whenever this occurred, the surveillance team was under strict instructions to alert the Governor. He would then visit the observation post located in the mountains some forty minutes away in his Landrover.

In May 2001 a minor member of the royal family was on a two day official visit to Valleymous on the Royal Yacht Britannia which was moored offshore.

These visits were a rare occurrence and aroused much interest on the part of the islanders. During the first day, the member of the royal family and his entourage were driven round the island during the course of which they made formal visits to the Woman's Institute, the Constabulary and the Boy Scouts. The second day was taken up by a reception in the grounds of Government House and a formal dinner in the evening.

During the course of the dinner, the Governor was alerted that the volcano was causing concern and his presence was required. He explained the circumstances to his royal guest who immediately understood the urgency and urged him to leave at once.

While still in formal evening attire, he was driven by his chauffeur to the observation post considerably irritated that the royal dinner of which he was the host had had to proceed without his presence and that the Deputy Governor would have the privilege of reading his speech.

On arrival at the observation post, he was met by a young engineer who guided him into the hut which acted as the control centre.

Immediately the governor announced:

—You have two minutes to explain your emergency call as I have more important matters on hand. I am entertaining royalty.

Somewhat daunted by the Governor's preamble, the young engineer explained the significance of the changing patterns on the monitor. The engineer was on his first assignment after leaving university and was nervous in the presence of such an august figure as His Excellency. He stammered and stuttered but was shown little understanding.

—Young man! —The Governor exploded— could you not have waited until the morning and informed my secretary? Do you not think that you could have shown better judgement than ask for my presence in the middle of the night to give me this technical assessment? I cannot see how you can justify your decision when the whole island knows I am hosting a dinner for a member of the royal family.

Humbled and embarrassed the engineer apologized and the Governor ordered the chauffeur to take him back to Government House. On his return, he found that the royal party, as a precautionary measure, had been advised to return by launch to the royal yacht which had now set sail to the next island on the tour.

At 4.00 a.m. the volcano erupted, the boy was killed, the population was further devastated but the Governor went to his bed angry that his moment of glory had been spoilt by the impetuosity of an inexperienced young engineer.

Trousers

Jim Sparkes was born in 1927 in Bradford to a working class family at the time of the Great Depression.

His parents were hard working and endowed with a puritan ethic. Life was to be endured and this was best achieved through routine and discipline. The father who laboured in a railway goods yard always left home at 7.00 in the morning and, whatever the weather, walked to and from work arriving back at 6.30 in the evening.

Most evenings after his supper he would read the local newspaper or listen to the radio cosseted round a coal fire in the winter but in the summer would spend his evenings tending a small allotment where he grew vegetables.

Mary, his wife was a frail lady devoted to her modest home which she only left to do the shopping and visit her close friend, Peggy, who lived across the street. She was rarely without her apron and her great joy in life was keeping the house spotless.

Their lives were governed by routine and the need to take account of the depressed economic times. The husband was very aware that he was fortunate to be in work and his ambition was simply to be debt free and secure. Holidays and other outings were a rarity.

Jim their only child was timid and introspective. He did not mix easily with the other boys, his main pursuits being stamp collecting and reading comics. He attended the local state primary school where he did well. The headmaster recognized that he was more interested in his studies than many of the other students and suggested to his parents that he take the Eleven Plus exam which, if he were to pass, would give him the opportunity to attend the local state grammar school.

At first his parents did not grasp the significance of the headmaster's recommendation fearing that this elevated educational environment was alien to their working class background and perhaps, more importantly, might involve financial outlays which they considered they could not afford.

The headmaster, however, recognized these working class prejudices and took the trouble to encourage Jim's parents to make the right decision. He explained that it would be a pity to waste a gifted child by not allowing him to take the chance of improving his circumstances.

Jim duly passed the entrance exam and during the course of the next few years did well gaining a state scholarship to Bradford University where he studied engineering. He now moved in a new world of middle-class values which distanced him from his parents and his background. As an undergraduate, in keeping with his character, he had studied long and hard without being distracted by the more adolescent student activities.

On graduating and obtaining his first job as an apprentice in a local engineering firm, his parents thought that the moment was right for him to settle down and get married. Their thinking was partly in line with their traditions but also in the hope that he would remain true to his roots.

As a shy and dutiful son he was vulnerable to the pressure of his parents who had in mind marriage to the daughter of his mother's best friend from across the street.

Peggy's daughter was called Pam. She was two years younger than Jim and was much sought after by the local lads all of whom had been working in "blue collar" jobs since they left school at sixteen or seventeen. She liked to be frivolous which included teasing her many admirers and generally being the centre of attention. She also considered that Jim was a bore and, now as a university graduate, a "toff" which made him still less attractive. She was far too interested in being taken to dances with other boys, some of whom had acquired motor bikes, a great status symbol at the time. By contrast, Jim with his quiet and introspective nature was not gregarious and in addition had never been particularly fond of Pam whom he had known since childhood.

Nevertheless, by dint of effort on the part of the two mothers, the couple eventually became engaged and married. Jim with his new status as a professional engineer was able to obtain a mortgage and the couple set up home in a newly built private estate in a more salubrious and middle-class part of town.

* * *

Ten years later in 1966, more through commitment and hard work than natural talent, Jim was made a director of his firm. He was then thirty six. I at the time was twenty five and working in Brazil. He had been sent out to Sao Paulo where we met. This was his first business trip abroad and we were to accompany each other during the month that he was there.

I had never before spent much time on a one-to-one basis with someone whom I considered, given the age diffwerence, was more adult than myself and presumably more familiar with the ways of the world. I was surprised therefore how during the long evenings we were obliged to spend together the extent to which he revealed intimate details about his life and marriage. These centred on the difficulty that he had relating to people in general, the strained relations with his parents and, most strangely, the unsatisfactory sexual relationship with his wife.

As a much younger single man, I was both intrigued and embarrassed by these revelations. It transpired that he needed to talk as he had no-one in whom he could confide back home. His parents were unsophisticated and his wife lacked depth and understanding. Further, in spite of his now elevated position as a director of an engineering firm, he felt, because of his roots, socially inferior to the other members of the board.

I like to think of myself as sympathetic to other people's difficulties and, if I can help, I am usually pleased to do so. Jim explained that he had chosen to confide in me as he felt that I was worldlier than him and, as he was far from home, whatever he said would not get back to Bradford. It was then that I understood my role was to listen.

He was distressed and frustrated by his inability to communicate with his parents, his childhood friends and the unsympathetic nature of his wife. He felt that he was caught between two worlds, the humble security of his working class origins and the current need to relate to the middle class values of ambition and social advancement.

In the course of these revelations he quite openly expressed the view that these frustrations might well disappear, or become more tolerable, if his wife were to show more interest in arousing him sexually but being lazy and indifferent she preferred to lounge around the house in trousers. Jim thought the explanation for this was that she in turn missed the emotional comforts and security that she had had during her childhood; the fact that she had married under pressure from her parents; and, that she was shunned by the other wives on the estate as a social upstart. He went on to add that he craved her affection. The stress was making him more introspective and less communicative.

I was asked my advice and, as I did not feel competent to reply, I enquired if there was anything that could be done which might change the situation. He explained that before they were married Pam used to take great care of her appearance to the point of being excessively provocative. He used to be aroused by this and it greatly attracted him although he soon realized that dressing in this way was not necessarily with him in mind. She relished the attention she received but now that she was married and living in a middle class environment where she felt mocked for her style, she felt isolated and had withdrawn into herself.

At this point, I was still not clear what he hoped could be done to improve the situation but eventually he came out with the suggestion of surprising his wife by buying her some provocative lingerie. He requested my help with the purchase on the grounds that I knew a little Portuguese to his none. I was uncomfortable but realized that this was a double call for help; namely, to assist him over his shyness and the practical aspects of making the purchase.

We went to the most expensive departmental store in Sao Paulo and found our way to the lingerie department. Through sign language Jim earnestly explained what he was looking for much to the amusement of the young sales assistant. Initially, she was haughty and disdainful but, on realizing his bashfulness and earnestness, became sympathetic and went out of her way to show him discreetly what he was looking for. Meanwhile, I sat on a chair at the end of the counter trying to avert the surprised glances of the smart looking customers as they passed by.

After about half an hour which seemed like an eternity, Jim opened his brief case and appeared to pay a large sum of money in cash. The items were first folded in tissue and then packaged in expensive wrapping paper.

As we left the store, Jim appeared highly excited and pleased with his purchases and I could not resist asking why he had paid what appeared a large sum in cash. He explained that he could not use a credit card lest his wife discover how much he had paid. I then realized that he had planned well in advance this once in a lifetime chance to indulge in this sexual fantasy and the opportunity to reconnect with his wife.

A few days later Jim had to return to the UK and after this bonding experience I was sure that I would hear from him again. Meanwhile, I found myself reflecting on the unusual relationship. In many ways it was both a maturing and alarming experience. As a young man in my mid twenties I was still adolescent in my sexual feelings and thought that with maturity that they would in time diminish and not produce the same emotional and physical stresses that were apparent in Jim. With the benefit of hindsight how wrong I was!

* * *

Two months elapsed and thoughts of Jim were receding into the past when I unexpectedly received a letter from a Roy Watson, a work colleague of Jim's.

The letter explained that Jim had been granted two months' leave of absence on compassionate grounds and that he, Roy Watson, would be taking over from Jim the firm's interest in the Brazil project. Enclosed with the letter was a cutting from a local newspaper.

The article was about a strange happening on a private residential estate in which a wife was having an affair with a neighbour's husband. The husband's wife discovered the affair and was so distressed that she took her own life. The husband was left with two young children.

The event caused such a local scandal that the husband felt obliged to give up his job and move to another part of the country. His lover accompanied him.

Professional integrity

Bray, situated to the south of Dublin on the east coast of Ireland, is now a busy commuter town but in the 1960s before the great economic expansion of Ireland was a small village.

At that time, there was only one store and it acted as general grocer and post office. Now nearly fifty years later, Bray is a dormitory town for workers from the big city.

Before the expansion, few people who worked in the capital lived in Bray as it was considered too far out of town and those that did commute were from the comfortably off professional classes. One such family was the Murphys, founders of the well known Dublin firm of solicitors bearing the same name.

In the 1960s, Mr. Desmond Murphy was the senior partner following the death of his father who had founded the firm in the 1920s. Like his father, he was successful and much respected in Irish society.

Mr. Murphy was the head of a large and united family. In spite of his high profile and the pressures of his profession, he always made sure that his home-life was kept private.

In this small community everyone knew each other, and as often as not, each others' business. People would meet everyday when taking their children to the local school, in church on Sundays or when shopping in the general store.

Siobhan O'Hara, the lady who owned the store, knew everything that went on in the community and frequently heard information for which discretion was needed. She was one of the best known characters in the village. She was always helpful, particularly with the elderly, and went out of her way to be kind and thoughtful. In addition, she somehow also found time to be on the local council and active in church affairs. She was considered approachable with a cheerful disposition and well loved by the less advantaged to whom she frequently provided advice on such matters as remedies for minor ills, recipes and help in form filling for those wishing to complete driving licence applications or other government documents.

Thus, the business of the store was the focal point of the village and its business extended beyond the provision of everyday food and consumables to a meeting point; a place to settle utility and other bills; and, as local post office and telephone exchange.

Mr. Desmond, as Mr. Murphy was known by the locals, was universally regarded as someone to be respected even though perhaps a little remote because of his elevated social position. This remoteness was not encouraged by him as he was fond of the villagers and could be counted upon to help in an emergency. Such help included discreet subsidy of medical bills for the less well-off, financial support for the local rugby team and an annual contribution towards the costs of the harvest festival. He frequently mixed with the villagers after Mass on Sundays and delighted in sharing a joke on occasional visits to the pub for a pint of Guinness.

Mr. Desmond was very punctilious and disciplined. These characteristics were not only in his nature but were born of the demands of his business and family. His business required him to be in the office by 8.30 a.m., a half hour drive from his home, and he always aimed to be back at the house by 6.30 p.m. in time to have a relaxing drink with those of his six children who might be present. In the mid 1960s, his children were either in their late teens or early twenties. There was always a lot happening and he took a keen interest, particularly in their sporting achievements having once been a keen sportsman himself.

Mr. Desmond especially looked forward to Fridays when he was able to participate in his own passions of golf and horse-racing. He was a member of the Irish Turf Club, the prestigious equestrian club founded in 1790, and was frequently to be seen in the Members' Enclosure at the Curagh. As a busy person, time was precious and arriving back at the house at the beginning of the week-end was a particularly joyous moment.

On one occasion, he walked through the front door at 6.30 p.m. on a Friday and, as he was hanging his hat and coat in the hall, the telephone rang. His wife who was beside him answered the telephone and informed him that it was Cyril O'Sullivan, a close personal friend and fellow member of the Turf Club. He imagined that Cyril would want to talk about the week-end racing and consequently was somewhat surprised when Cyril started to press him on an urgent legal matter. Feeling compromised between wishing to oblige a friend and his strict routine of not dealing with business matters from home, he startled his friend by replying sharply:

—Cyril, I am always pleased to hear from you and I am looking forward to our meeting over the week-end but I regret that on principle I refuse to talk business on the telephone from home. There are three reasons for this. Firstly, I have only just walked through the door and am not thinking about work; secondly, whatever I advise cannot be acted upon until Monday as all businesses will be closed for the week-end; and, thirdly and most importantly, the little old lady at the local store always listens in.

Whereupon the voice of Siobhan was heard to interject:

—Upon my word, I never!

Cyril laughed and immediately understood.

The interview

At the end of each scholastic year, many large multinational companies send senior personnel to the leading universities in search of new recruits. The annual intake of undergraduates can in the case of the many international organizations number in the hundreds. It is therefore viewed as an important exercise and an opportunity to attract the most able students.

These tours take place towards the end of the academic year and any student identified as a promising candidate is usually offered a further interview on the understanding that he obtains a good grade in his final exam.

Not all students are bothered to meet the companies' representatives since they are pre-occupied in preparations for their final exam. Nevertheless, the more ambitious and confident take the time out in the hope of securing an opportunity with a top flight company.

One such student was Charles Brown, a very self-assured young man recognized by his peers as someone with great confidence, ability and ambition.

Charles was also aware that great things were expected of him and he had little doubt that he would succeed in whatever he undertook.

As expected, Charles obtained his degree with good grades and on informing the three companies that had invited him to seek an interview, he duly contacted them.

One of the companies was Unilever, the international food and household products group who on receiving confirmation of his exam results honoured its undertaking and invited him to the first round of interviews at its head office. He duly arrived on the appointed day and to his surprise discovered that up to three hundred other recent graduates from universities from all over the country had also been invited. He was further surprised to learn that he would be asked to take a written general knowledge test apparently designed to assess his aptitude. He took the written test and was advised that he would be notified in due course as to whether he had been short-listed for the next round of selection. He left for home somewhat bemused as he found the test trivial. He took it for certain that he would be asked to the next round.

Several days later he received a letter from the company inviting him to return. He again presented himself and on this occasion found that the number of applicants was now down to fifty and that there were just thirty vacancies.

When all the candidates had assembled, they were shown into a large conference hall and Charles was surprised to note that at one end of this large area were five rows of chairs and at the other end a table with just six seats. There was a huge open space in the middle and a double door halfway down to one side.

The recruits waited in their seats until the double doors were opened whereupon they stood up and watched six men carrying folders file in and sit down at the table at the other end of the room. Charles and the other aspirants sniggered amongst themselves at what seemed a comic procession. The arrivals were all directors.

The Director of Personnel chaired the meeting. Firstly, he introduced his fellow directors and then gave a short history of the company, its products and future aspirations. He explained that they were now looking to recruit thirty graduates for its marketing division. The procedure would be that every candidate would be called up individually and would be asked questions by each of the directors.

He then referred to his folder and called out the first name:

—Would Mr. Charles Brown please make himself known?

Charles stood up.

—Mr. Brown, please step forward.

Charles stood up and walked towards the centre of the hall. He felt a little foolish but did as he was instructed. He was not overly impressed with the procedure and wondered what this was all about. As he reached the centre of the open space, he was asked to stop. It was at this point he was getting annoyed.

After he had stopped, there was a short pause after which the Director of Personnel said:

—Mr. Brown, entertain us for a few minutes.

Charles was now seething and was singularly unimpressed with the procedure. He also imagined that whatever he said would be a disaster and concluded that it was better to give up all hope of acquiring the job and walk away.

Disappointed and angered, he put on a brave face and said:

—There must be some mistake. I came thinking that I was coming for an interview and not for an audition as a cabaret act.

Thereupon he walked swiftly to the double doors at the side of the hall. As he was about to leave, the Director of Personnel shouted at him to wait. He stopped and glared at the director.

—Mr. Brown, congratulations you have got the job!

Delayed gratitude

On one of my occasional visits to an aunt who lived in Belgravia, I was asked whether I would like to accompany her to a presentation at Fowles Bookshop. The aunt enjoyed London social life and was to be seen at many of the big occasions. Her husband, now retired, was delighted when I accepted the invitation as he was not too fond of these events and preferred to stay at home.

Like her husband, I was not fond of these occasions either but I considered that it was expected of me and I was pleased to accompany her. This aunt had also long been preoccupied that I was now middle aged and had been on my own for nearly twenty years. She would never admit to it but it was on her mind that I might meet a prospective partner. Furthermore, she could not understand my not wishing to be social and move in London society, a world in which she thought all "civilized" people should be eager to participate.

On arrival at the reception, the guests, which must have numbered a hundred, were busy chatting and reaching out for drinks from one of the passing waiters. In the overcrowded and overly warm atmosphere everyone was doing their utmost to carry on a "civilized" exchange but it appeared difficult when, as likely as not, they did not know the person to whom they were talking; they could hardly hear above the noise, while at the same time, trying to attract the attention of a waiter or greet an acquaintance sighted at the other side of the room.

On entering the hall, my aunt was quickly engaged with greetings to a number of acquaintances and I then realized that I was on my own.

I have always been a little awkward in these sophisticated environments and after a few greetings and an exchange about nothing of any consequence, I did not get the feeling that I was making much impression. After each brief encounter, everyone seemed anxious to move on.

The occasion appeared pretentious with questionable motives on the part of the sponsors and the invited, the sponsors being motivated by commercial expectations and the guests by a contrived *bonhomie*.

At one stage, I found myself talking to an attractive Chilean lady and given her appearance and style, I felt out of my league. She nevertheless listened, no doubt with feigned interest, at my attempt to be sociable and, after a lengthy but forgettable conversation, I was surprised when she invited me to a dinner party at her home in Chelsea scheduled for a few days later.

I accepted.

The Chilean lady had at one time been married to a British businessman who a few years previously had been killed in a plane crash and had left her well provided for. In the circumstances knowing that she had everything, I had difficulty deciding what would be an acceptable gift. I eventually decided on a fine bottle of Chilean wine. I sought advice from a wine merchant who suggested that if I wanted the wine to be appreciated by a *connoisseur* of Chilean wines, then he recommended a red wine called "Le Dix de los Vascos 1996". I accepted the advice and duly made the purchase. It cost a great deal more than I had anticipated but I considered it necessary at the time.

On the appointed day, I arrived at the door and was met by a uniformed manservant who immediately relieved me of my gift and my overcoat. I was then ushered into the drawing-room and my name was announced to the assembled party. The hostess quickly came forward to welcome me and I was introduced to a South American gentleman who spoke little English, but somewhat more than my Spanish. We struggled to exchange pleasantries. After the pre-dinner drinks, we were shown into an elegant dining-room where I was surprised to find myself seated next to the hostess one side and an ambassador's wife on the other.

The conversation ranged from the problem of obtaining servants (they were either very expensive or did not speak English); to plans for coordinating the summer visits of guests to their holiday homes on the Riviera; to the difficulty in obtaining tickets for the forthcoming visit of Rudolf Nureyev to Sadler's Wells; and, to the absurdity of the new parking regulations passed by the Kensington and Chelsea Borough Council.

I listened attentively and tried to contribute with accounts of my experiences working overseas. At the mention of having recently returned from the Middle East, there was limited interest but it did include a comment to the effect how noisy their Arab neighbours could be and how their presence in Chelsea was affecting the price of property.

After dinner, we returned to the drawing-room where we formed several groups of three or four, the ladies seated for the most part while the men stood balancing a cup of coffee or a liqueur in one hand and an After Eight or other sweet delicacy in the other.

The ladies seemed relieved to be free from the more formal conversation at the dinner table and pleased to be talking amongst themselves on matters of interest to them, while the men were busy discussing the latest goings-on in politics and the business world. The sardonic exchanges between the men appeared designed to reflect their knowingness and sophistication.

Finally, the moment arrived for the guests to express their appreciation for the wonderful dinner and interesting conversation.

Many months later when I had long forgotten the reception at Fowles and the Chilean lady's dinner party, my aunt invited me to lunch at her house. This happened once in a while and was not out of the ordinary.

To my surprise, the Chilean lady was one of the other guests. As I entered the room, she came to greet me.

—Oh, how nice to see you again! —She said— I have wanted to thank you for your thoughtful gift on the occasion of my dinner party. It was so kind of you to bring such lovely chocolates.

Mixing with royalty

The late Emir of Bahrain, Sheikh Isa bin Salman al-Khalifa, ruled the country from 1961 to 1999 when he collapsed suddenly and died of a heart attack. He was just 65.

At his funeral, in accordance with local custom, he was buried within hours of his death. So popular was the Sheikh that on the announcement of his death on television, ten thousand people are estimated to have been at his grave-side for the burial in Rifaa, some distance from the capital, while a further fifty thousand lined the streets to pay their respects.

Bahrain is a small island state in the Gulf, only a short distance offshore from Saudi Arabia. In the 1930s, it was the first country in the region to discover oil but, by the standards of later discoveries, only modest in amount and extraction was already on the decline at the time that Sheikh Isa came to power.

The Sheikh's popularity was due in part to his domestic and foreign policies which he maintained in the face of opposition at home and abroad, especially from his powerful neighbours, Iran and Iraq.

After independence, he entered into a treaty with Britain and maintained a pro-Western stance allowing the British and US military to be stationed on the island. This policy helped preserve the country from its neighbours.

With diminishing oil revenues, the Emir embarked on political and economic reforms which at the time were considered controversial. These committed the country to Western ideas, including an elected Parliament in 1973. The Parliament, however, was later suspended because of extremists. At the same time, he sought to retain the country's cultural and Islamic roots.

The economic projects involved the largest aluminium smelter in the region, a dry dock and an international banking centre all of which had the effect of making the country a regional service and business centre.

The success of these measures resulted in Bahrain having a different character from its neighbours. Bahrain developed the highest literary rate in the Arab world, created an educated middle-class that competed with Westerners in a number of occupations and a liberal culture with a multi-faith environment.

In addition to these achievements, the Emir's great popularity with his people and foreigners was the result of his personal warmth, common touch and renowned sense of humour. He was known for the twinkle in his eye, especially in the presence of an attractive lady, and he invariably greeted newcomers with the words:-

—Welcome to Bahrain! And I hope my people are making you feel at home.

Every two weeks on a Tuesday, he used to hold an open Court---a *Majlis*---at which citizens and foreigners could approach him on any matter and submit petitions. There are many recorded accounts where individuals have been helped in ways they least expected. He is believed to have wished to be seen as provider, protector and friend.

This mixture of astute leadership and approachability combined with his sense of humour were his hallmarks.

* * *

Mervyn Oram was a British banker working on a long-term contract in Bahrain. Like most expatriate workers he had a busy social life which included eating out in a diverse range of international restaurants, drinks in the bars of the principal hotels, membership of the Bankers Club with its sporting facilities and visits to the Sheikh's Beach.

To any Westerner who has lived in Bahrain, a visit to the Sheikh's Beach is a must. It is some distance out of Manama, the capital, and is the private property of the Emir. It is a beauty spot which fronts onto a pristine sandy beach and is surrounded by a walled-garden. Once inside the property, the approach to the beach through the gardens leads to a tarmac parking area with the Emir's beach house on the left and a wooden jetty in front. Westerners have free access to the beach on the understanding they will respect local customs. When alive, the Emir used to frequent the beach on Fridays, the Muslim day off, and very much enjoyed talking to whoever approached him.

Mervyn Oram was a bachelor and had a spoilt existence which included a car, a large villa with swimming pool and a servant who came each day, all of which were paid for by his employer. Each February, he used to invite his mother, Idina Oram, to stay for a month. She lived in the UK and, as she was a widow and lived on her own, this was the highlight of her year.

Many of Mervyn's social activities had to be curtailed while his mother was staying; but they both enjoyed the swimming pool and the outings to restaurants.

On one occasion in the course of conversation, Mervyn mentioned the possibility of making a visit the Sheikh's Beach. His mother enquired what this entailed and why it would be special. Mervyn explained that the beach was private; that it belonged to the ruling family; and that, if they were to go on a Friday, there was a possibility of meeting the Emir.

Idina Oram was a sophisticated lady who in her youth in the 1930s had been a debutante during the London social season. Nevertheless, in spite of her worldliness, she was intrigued at the possibility of meeting the Emir. On the next Friday, a picnic was prepared and stowed into the boot of the car with a well stocked cooler. The drive took about forty minutes and Mervyn and Idina arrived at midday, still in time to secure a parking spot in the central parking area next to the Emir's beach house, in a reality a small ornate marble palace.

The beach was accessible on both sides of the parking area and Mervyn and Idina chose to go to the right as it was likely to be quieter. The picnic was laid out and enjoyed after which Idina socked up the sun and had a swim. Mervyn sensed that she was wondering whether it was true what he had told her about meeting the Emir and he explained that he usually did not arrive before three in the afternoon and that nearer the time they would stroll to where he usually sat.

Idina was now in her sixties but still retained her feminine vanity and was self-conscious about being in a swimsuit. By three o'clock, she was already hot and sticky from the heat and was feeling uncomfortable when Mervyn announced that the time had come when the Emir would be on the beach. They walked back towards the parking area next to the summer house and were passing between the line of cars when Idina enquired:

—Mervyn, I cannot see any Emir here.

Mervyn was embarrassed at such forthrightness and was about to hush her when from behind a nearby car a voice called out:

—Here I am!

At this point Idina blushed becoming still redder and was feeling uncomfortable standing in her swimsuit as the Emir appeared from between the cars. He was dressed in a fine white Egyptian cotton *dish-dash* with embroidered lace.

The Emir who was very conversant with British ways sized up the situation immediately and gallantly tried to put her at her ease.

—I imagine that you have only recently arrived and have come out to Bahrain to visit your son who must be working here. Welcome to Bahrain! And I hope that my people are treating you well.

Idina was instantly charmed and made to feel relaxed. They exchanged pleasantries and then he invited her to tea. She of course accepted and he guided her between the cars to a terraced area just outside the entrance to his beach house.

Mervyn followed behind and when the Emir noticed his continued presence asked him to return later as he wanted to have a private conversation with his mother. He invited Idina to sit down at a table where there were two chairs. He then snapped his fingers and a uniformed servant appeared. He gave instructions for tea to be served and Idina could not help but notice the teabags hanging out of the top of the silver teapot.

The conversation was lively as Idina soon got over her shyness. She was surprised how conversant the Emir was with every day happenings in the UK and she was particularly interested to learn that he owned a stud farm in Sussex which he frequented on private visits to the UK. From talk about the stud farm, the conversation turned to horses which happened to be a great passion for both of them. This was followed by talk about the Queen's horses during which the Emir revealed that he spoke to her occasionally in private over the telephone. Idina was surprised and enchanted at such apparent confidences which prompted her to enquire when he last saw her. The Emir replied:

—As a matter of fact, Her Majesty came on a state visit to Bahrain only a year ago and, on one of the days she was here, we walked along this beach in the cool of the evening.

—Oh, how very interesting! I am sure that she must also have enjoyed the location.

—Yes, I believe she did. Her Majesty is always very gracious and I enjoy the times when we can meet.

—I expect that you had a lot to talk about.

—Yes, especially when the formal business was concluded. Her Majesty has a great sense of humour and we always laugh about many things.

—That sounds intriguing —Idina replied.

—As a matter of fact, —The Emir continued— on the last occasion she was here when we were walking along this beach, she asked me when I was next coming to England.

—And may I ask how you replied?

—Of course. I enquired of Her Majesty. "Ma'am, do you not already have you enough *bloody* foreigners without me?"

An unequal exchange

On returning to the UK with my family after having spent a long period abroad, we spent our vacation in a hotel in London. The hotel was located on the north side of Hyde Park and was close to the well-known shopping centre of Oxford Street.

In the mid 1970s when the price of oil increased nearly fourfold, London was full of tourists from the Middle East keen to spend their new found wealth on massive shopping sprees. Our hotel was full of such tourists.

At the time we had a year old son and my wife, not unnaturally, was finding it difficult to look after him in the impersonal surroundings of a hotel. In order not to have to stay in the confines of the room, she would spend long periods in the lobby and social areas of the hotel.

On one occasion she got into conversation with an Iranian lady who was travelling on her own and who spoke very little English. My wife soon realized that she was a little lost on her first visit abroad and offered to accompany her one afternoon to show her how to get to Oxford Street and to locate the better known shops. The Iranian lady readily accepted.

The lady was probably in her early forties, a little overweight and heavily made-up. She dressed extravagantly and it was apparent that she had once been attractive but had let herself go. She had an excessively over-confident manner, doubtless the result of having been much sought after my men in her younger years. My wife who had spent her youth in Iran and was familiar with the language and culture was surprised to find an Iranian lady without a companion. Ladies from the Middle East rarely travelled alone, especially abroad.

On the day my wife accompanied her to Oxford Street, the two took a taxi and toured the shops. My wife's companion was very demanding and, in spite of her apparent social background, treated my wife as though she was in her employ.

Exhausted and irritated by the insensitivity and egoist manner, my wife suggested that they stopped for lunch to which the other agreed. In the restaurant, the Iranian lady talked about her life and she related that in Teheran she had been in "high society" and had made a speciality in arranging introductions to the rich and powerful. She was apparently in the confidence of the establishment and was relied upon for her discretion. Nevertheless, she felt politically vulnerable because many of the men for whom she had made introductions now feared being portrayed by an indiscretion. As the risks and tensions grew she became more and more aware of her vulnerability and had decided to retire. She also wanted to leave Iran permanently but was having difficulty deciding where to settle and how to go about it.

Although she did not speak English she had chosen to come to the UK because she had been provided in Teheran with an introduction to an agent who arranged marriages of convenience for those seeking to acquire a British passport. The agent was of Iranian origin and was believed to have already brokered a number of such transactions. Prior to coming to London, she had been in communication with this person and a preliminary proposal had already been discussed. It involved a contract whereby she would marry an aged English widower in his seventies, thereby obtaining through marriage the legal right to apply for citizenship and a UK passport. One of the conditions of the marriage contract would be a provision that after the civil ceremony, the couple would go their separate ways never to meet again. The agent would be paid £10,000 which included an unknown amount payable to the aged widower. In the hope of facilitating the process, the lady, in all seriousness, sought my wife's help in finding an English lawyer.

My wife was nonplussed by these revelations and determined to bring the acquaintance to a rapid close. The bill was settled and she took a taxi back to the hotel leaving the lady to continue to tour the shops. For the next few days, my wife did everything possible not to bump into her in the lobby, but during the course of a two week stay it proved difficult.

Several days later there was a disturbance in the lobby as the Iranian lady, in a highly hysterical state, was being accompanied by, we were to learn later, a plain clothed policeman. The two were standing in front of the reception desk and the policeman was enquiring whether there was anyone in the hotel acquainted with the lady as the police at the station were unable to communicate with her in her language. The desk clerk said that she was known to be travelling alone but since her arrival had befriended another guest. This was a reference to my wife who was duly asked if she would mind coming down to the lobby.

When my wife arrived the policeman asked the reception clerk whether there was somewhere where they could have a private conversation and the three were ushered into the empty manager's office.

The policeman then explained that the lady had been caught on camera stealing in Marks and Spencers, the well-known high street departmental store and had been apprehended on leaving the premises and taken to the Marylebone Police Station. She had been formally charged with theft and was required to appear in the Magistrate's Court the following day at 10.00 a.m. He was most concerned that the lady should understand what was happening and the need for her to be present in court. He also explained that she would be provided on arrival at the court with an English lawyer and an Iranian interpreter.

My wife tried to explain the gravity of the situation to the lady and that she had no option but to comply. The lady was very indignant, distraught and confused and implored my wife to accompany her. Reluctantly, she agreed on humane grounds realizing that she was her only contact and means of support in this strange land.

The following day the Iranian lady accompanied by my wife arrived at the Magistrate's Court where they were met by the same policeman, this time dressed in his uniform. He thanked my wife for supporting the lady and escorted both of them to a waiting-room outside the court. There the lady was introduced to the lawyer appointed to act on her behalf and to the Iranian interpreter. The Iranian lady tried to enlist the sympathy and support of the interpreter but he explained very firmly that he was being engaged to act as a court interpreter and that there was no way he might "fix" the outcome of the hearing. The Iranian lady rebuked him as a traitor for not coming to the aid of a defenceless compatriot in a moment of need.

Once the hearing got underway, there was the formal prosecution presented by the lawyer representing the store followed by that of the court appointed defence lawyer. Both presentations were simultaneously translated through headphones to the defendant by the interpreter who was situated in a sound-proofed cabin at the side of the court. As is normal in these proceedings, the magistrate subsequently asked for clarification of a few details and then explained to the defendant the law governing the charge.

The Iranian lady did not appear impressed and was disdainful of the attempt by the magistrate to show an even-handed understanding of the incident. Her outrage was only contained by the gestures of her lawyer who was trying to convey in hand signals that she needed to be more in control and that her tantrum would not help her cause. The lawyer's efforts were largely ignored.

On completion of the magistrate's summing-up, there was a short interlude while he called both legal representatives to the bar. There was a whispered conversation between three of them and it can only be assumed that, in spite of the evidence, the magistrate was perhaps seeking a way to diminish the impact of a guilty decision to mollify the defendant and take into account that the theft was petty, impetuous and unnecessary.

On completion of his consultation with the lawyers, the magistrate ordered them to return to their seats, whereupon the court was asked to be upstanding. He then read out his decision in which he found the defendant guilty as charged. However, before passing sentence he asked the lady if she had anything to say in explanation before passing sentence.

The lady, who at this point was overcome with rage, rose to her feet and angrily shouted at the magistrate:-

—Why all this fuss over a pair of gloves when you have been stealing our oil for years?

Why me?

For a number of years while bringing up my family, I lived in London and commuted to my work from the suburb of Blackheath. The suburb is one of the leafiest areas of Greater London with tree lined streets, private estates and several large open spaces, including of course the heath and Greenwich Park. The area used to be, and I imagine still is, favoured by young professionals, especially for some reason by those that work in the media and academia.

In addition to open spaces, Blackheath is known for the excellence of its state and private schools and these amenities have no doubt played an important part in attracting middle-class parents ambitious for the education of their children.

At the time, I imagine that my wife and I must have had the same thoughts for on our return from working overseas, we opted to buy a house and set up home in the area.

After living there a few weeks, I returned home one evening to find my wife excited at having made a new friend. Initially, and not altogether surprisingly, she had felt lonely having only recently arrived from overseas and not knowing anyone in the area. Young children, however, like owning a pet, can often be a better source of making connections than attending a party. In this case, my wife had taken our four year old son for a walk in Greenwich Park to play on the swings and, while minding him, had got into conversation with the mother of girl of the same age as our son. While the children played, the mothers talked.

As the afternoon progressed, Mary Williams, for that was the other mother's name, invited my wife to tea. My wife explained that she would like to accept but she did not yet have a car and would not be able to get home easily, whereupon Mary agreed to take her home afterwards. This unexpected need to extend the invitation to providing a lift no doubt helped contribute to the bonding. In short, it was the beginning of a long friendship.

The tea took place in the Mary's kitchen while the children played at teasing the cat.

Both Mary and my wife found themselves in a similar situation as young mothers with children of the same age and had much to talk about, including their husbands. Mary's husband was a professor of economics at the London School of Economics and my wife thought it would be interesting if the husbands were to meet. The outcome was that we remained in regular contact.

The husband was called Thomas Williams. He was a little eccentric in a charmingly academic sort of way and not given to socializing, preferring at all times to be in his study. He did, however, have a good sense of humour and, of course, we were both fathers with children of the same age which meant we had something in common. Above all, like me, he seemed pleased to see his wife make a new friend.

Over time, the wives became very close and exchanged confidences. Mary used to complain that one of her biggest difficulties with Thomas was to get him to help about the house, as might be expected of a middle-class suburban husband. Like me, Thomas had two left hands when it came to decorating or hanging a picture and was not focused on being practical.

Mary and Thomas were a devoted couple but Mary explained that she did not have the time nor the patience to oversee Thomas, as well as carry out the other household chores. She had long concluded that it was quicker and safer to do things herself. As a result, when she noticed that Thomas was anxious to return to his papers, she no longer complained nor discouraged him.

In the mornings, for example, Mary would prepare his breakfast and then let him get ready for work at his own pace while she concentrated on preparing her daughter for school. This became the regular morning pattern and, if he feared being late for the commuter train, he would call up from the bottom of the stairs and hurry off to the station.

Thomas was aware of his vagueness and absent-mindedness but was never bothered by what others thought providing he was not giving offence. He frequently recognized the other commuters but avoided socializing, whereas many of them had regular conversations or played cards.

On one such journey, he was minding his own business as usual and engrossed in reading the newspaper when he became aware that unwittingly he was attracting attention and receiving glances. He tried not to notice. Uncharacteristically, however, he was becoming self-conscious and decided to hurry off the train on arrival at the terminal.

For once he arrived at his office before his colleagues and thought that he should perhaps look at himself in the mirror. As he had never felt the need for a mirror in the office, he visited the men's room before anyone else arrived. He was pleased that he did, as to his amusement, and no doubt to that of his fellow passengers, he saw that he was wearing two ties.

A mysterious encounter

Frederick Harcourt qualified as an architect and as a member of the Royal Institute of Architecture in 1938 at the age of twenty seven. He had just started his first job with a private architectural practice when World War II broke out and he was called up. He joined the marines and was sent to Burma where he spent most of the war.

On being demobbed, he set about looking for work but in the post-war environment there were few opportunities for private architectural practice as the priority was the building of low cost housing. For a while he was able to find work with a firm that had been sub-contracted by the government. He stayed with the firm until the early part of the 1950s but concluded that in the current climate his chosen profession did not offer many opportunities.

After much thought, he decided to retrain as a town planner, a related activity which appeared to offer better career prospects. Many architects, it seems, had come to the same conclusion, consequently there was tough competition for the positions and the few openings that did exist were poorly paid. It was then that he decided to consider working overseas.

In the 1950s, the more advanced countries were not the only ones suffering from economic austerity and shortages; the Third World was also hurting. The richer nations were not in the position to offer aid and it was left to the United Nations, international charities and missionaries to help where they could.

After many disappointments, Frederick finally secured a two year appointment with UNESCO which required him to be based in Monrovia, the capital of Liberia in West Africa, where thousands were fleeing their village homes in search of food and work in the city. This migration was causing huge health, housing, infrastructure and utility supply problems.

Liberia is Africa's oldest republic and has an unusual history. It was founded by freed American and Caribbean slaves. Over a long period, their descendents made-up the political class although they only accounted for as little as five percent of the population. This situation has never made for harmony and explains the on-going unrest.

Frederick had never been to Africa and was apprehensive about the need to accept this position given the harshness of the West African climate and the remoteness of the location, especially as it would mean leaving behind his wife and young daughter. On the other hand, the lack of alternative opportunities required him to accept the offer. He had the feeling that he had only recently come back from war with all its privations and was now going to have to endure them again.

After a month of preparations which included medical check-ups, inoculations against malaria, yellow fever, hepatitis B and visits to tropical outfitters, he travelled to the Paris headquarters of UNESCO for his initial briefing and two days later he flew out to Monrovia on a Pan Am flight, the only international commercial airline flying to Liberia at the time.

On arrival at the airport he was shocked to see the crowds and the extreme poverty. He took a taxi to the most recommended hotel in town, The Ducal Palace, and exhausted by the journey and a little concerned as to how he was going to cope slumped into bed.

There were few foreigners in Liberia at the time and he was surprised to learn that even those working on a bachelor status rarely left the confines of the hotel except to go to their place of work. In addition to the poverty, they had been briefed on the insecurity and the lack of amenities.

His contract did not provide for his family to accompany him but, after two months, he decided that the boredom and the separation were too much and that he would invite his wife and daughter to join him having first explained the conditions. His wife was delighted and it was agreed that mother and daughter would travel out by ship to join him.

In the 1950s, the Union Castle Line was still operating the route between Southampton in the UK and Cape Town in South Africa with mail and refuelling stops on the way. A berth was booked on the "Arundel Castle" and Mrs. and Miss Harcourt were greatly excited by the prospect of travelling on a famous liner and escaping the post-war rationing and other restrictions still operating in Britain.

Life on board exceeded their expectations. During the day, they spent much of the time round the swimming pool and at night they enjoyed dressing-up for dances and participating in the organized entertainment.

The first port of call was Freetown in Sierra Leone where there was a six hour stopover. Many of the passengers were travelling to Cape Town to start a new life in South Africa and, as this was their first sight of the continent, most opted to spend two or three hours ashore. Mrs. Harcourt, however, decided that as they were unaccompanied, it would be prudent not to go ashore and so planned to spend the afternoon round the ship's swimming pool. As soon as she and her daughter had settled round the pool, there was an announcement over the public address system:-

—Would Mrs. Harcourt and her daughter please make their way to the Bursar's Office?

Surprised, they quickly dressed in a bathing wrap and went to see the Bursar. He informed them that he had been contacted by someone on the quay wishing to invite them to visit the town. The Bursar explained, as delicately as the situation permitted, that the man in question was a local and intimated that, unless they knew the gentleman, it might be wise to show caution in accepting an invitation. The Bursar also made them aware that, if they were to look discreetly over the side of the ship, they could see the man standing next to an open car.

Mrs. Harcourt was intrigued and on looking over the side saw a tall and very smartly dressed man standing next to an open top Cadillac. She assumed that he must be a colleague of her husband and that he had offered to meet them as a courtesy. After a moment's reflection she decided to accept. The gentleman was duly informed by the Bursar and asked to wait while Mrs. and Miss Harcourt got ready.

Half an hour later, they descended the gangplank where the gentleman was waiting. He introduced himself as Dr. Wachuku. He shook their hands and welcomed them to Sierra Leone. In the course of conversation, she was comforted to hear him say that he knew her husband and she had no reason to doubt him. He was very courteous and explained that he had spent many happy years as a student studying medicine at the London Hospital but since returning to Sierra Leone he had been so busy that he had not been able to leave the country. He seemed genuinely pleased to meet them and expressed great interest in showing them around Freetown.

Dr. Wachuku first took them to lunch at a French restaurant and then drove them to see the sights. Freetown is hilly and on a peninsular and at nearly every point there is a view of a sandy beach. Dr. Wachuku warmed to his role as tour guide and took them to see the famous Cotton Tree, reputed to be the site of a former slave market, The Slave Gate and St. George's Cathedral. They appreciated his continuous banter but were much more taken by the general atmosphere of their first encounter with Africa and the ride in the open top Cadillac.

About two hours before they were due back on board, Dr. Wachuku asked if he might buy them a present as a memento of their meeting. At this point they were walking round the open market which was intriguing them with its local colour and smells. He offered to buy her some jewellery

Mrs. Harcourt who was a sophisticated lady but with a bohemian streak had never been interested in jewellery and it was out of the question under any circumstances that she would accept such an offer from a stranger, however well intended. Just as she was again politely declining his offer, she caught sight on a nearby stall of a small wood carved statue of a nude lady seated on a stool. Partly out of genuine interest, but also to deflect Dr. Wachuku's insistence on jewellery, she mentioned how much she liked the carving. He was disdainful saying that it was a worthless piece of local art and that he had in mind something which he considered more worthy. After further lengthy but courteous exchanges, Mrs. Harcourt insisted that it would be the carving or nothing. He finally understood and made the purchase. She was genuinely delighted and said she could not have wished for a better memento of such a delightful meeting.

Dr. Wachuku then drove them back to the dock and fond farewells were exchanged at the foot of the gangplank. Mrs. Harcourt and her daughter had been genuinely thrilled with their first encounter with Africa and were looking forward to giving a long account of their adventure to Mr. Harcourt on arrival in Monrovia.

Two days later the ship docked in Monrovia where Mr. Harcourt was frantically trying to catch their attention from the quayside. After what seemed an interminable delay, they were finally able to identify their luggage, obtain the services of a porter and pass through customs. As they walked through the customs shed followed by the porters, they were duly met by Mr. Harcourt. There was an emotional reunion in the middle of the chaotic surroundings. Eventually, they reached the car and, after paying off the porters, Mr. Harcourt drove out of the airport trying as best he could to avoid running over the number of beggars who were chasing the car in the hope of a handout.

Once on the road to Monrovia, it became possible to carry on a normal conversation and one of the first questions Mrs. Harcourt asked:-

—Who was the charming doctor who was waiting on the dockside to meet us during the stopover in Freetown?

—What doctor are you talking about, my dear? — Replied Mr. Harcourt.

—Why? Dr. Wachuku, of course

—Dr. Wachuku? —He queried— I do not know a Dr. Wachuku.

—Surely, you do. He met us at the dockside in Freetown and took us out to lunch and sight-seeing during the few hours we were there.

—I have never known anyone of that name. Furthermore, I have never been to Freetown. You will recall I have only been in Monrovia a couple of months and flew here directly from Europe. I have been so busy that I have not even had a chance to see outside the city, let alone leave the country.

She had heard that Africa was a strange and different world, but she never found an explanation for the meeting and is frequently reminded of the encounter by the statue which continues to adorn the mantelpiece in her living-room.

A helping hand

Peter Fletcher was nineteen when he began his university studies as an undergraduate at Trinity College Dublin. At the end of his first term in 1962, he returned to London and to his home in Chelsea to spend Christmas with his family and to party.

Like most students, he was short of cash and decided to get a temporary job in the lead up to Christmas. He went to work as a postman at the regional sorting office in Chelsea Manor Street which was within walking distance of his home.

In the 1960s automated sorting of the mail did not exist and it was necessary for postmen to start early in order to prepare for their round. From 6.00 a.m. to 7.30 a.m. each postman sorted and bundled mail using specially designed shelves with pigeon holes which contained the street names and house numbers.

During the first few days, Peter was always slow in completing his sort but the professional postmen frequently came to his aide so that he would not be late setting off on his round.

By 7.30 all delivery postmen were expected to be on their way. This was particularly important over the Christmas period because of the seasonally high volume of mail. The work was physically demanding as each postman was required to make two rounds, one in the morning and the other in afternoon, and could not finish until these had been completed. The day frequently did not end until 4.00 p.m.

For someone who was in party mode the day seemed very long and at times Peter only managed to stay awake and keep up through the *bonhomie* of the fulltime workers and their willingness to lend a hand. They were never short of a joke and delighted in recounting unusual experiences delivering the mail.

At 7.30 a.m. after a short break which included a sustaining mug of hot sweet tea, the mailbags and their respective postman were taken by van and dropped off at the beginning of their round.

Peter's round started in Cheyne Walk. The street consists of elegant family residences overlooking the River Thames and the houses date from the late eighteenth century. As one of the most fashionable addresses in London, it has always been home to the well-to-do.

On the first day, Peter felt like Father Christmas as he struggled with an over large and heavenly laden sack. This thought was further compounded by the snow which was thick on the ground. It was still early in the morning, very cold and with a piercing wind.

In order to extract from his sack the first bundle for delivery he needed to find somewhere out of the snow and under cover. A short way down the street he saw a cobbled archway leading to the back of one of the houses. In former times, this had no doubt been the entrance to stables but was now a private parking area.

Peter hurried to the archway and was relieved to be out of the snow and sheltered from the wind. He emptied the mailbag onto the cobble stones, lined up the bundles and selected those for immediate delivery. Once he had selected the letters for Cheyne Walk, he was going to leave the mailbag under the arch while he made his first deliveries.

While on his knees arranging the bundles, Peter did not immediately notice the presence of someone else but as he looked up a letter took off in a gust of wind. The letter was only saved by the elderly gentleman standing under the archway who trapped it with his cane.

Peter was not sure how he would react and half expected a rebuke. Also, he was conscious that being responsible for the Royal Mail, he could, if reported, be instantly dismissed by the postal authorities for negligence and trespassing.

He reached across the cobbles to retrieve the letter from under the gentleman's cane.

—Young man, I can see you are not very experienced, would you like a hand? I know everyone who lives in this street.

Peter was relieved at his reaction and surprised when the gentleman bent over and pointed at one of the letters. He noted that the letter was addressed to Lord Iveagh.

—I will keep this one, it is addressed to me.

Peter was now flustered but appreciative of the gentle manner of this elderly gentleman who seemed keen to help and wanting to engage in conversation.

A conversation followed in which the gentleman explained that it was his custom whatever the weather to take a stroll before breakfast and that he liked to be up and about before the crowds. He also went on to explain that being retired he missed the discipline of work and that he had to be strict with himself not to become idle.

During this conversation he also explained to Peter which family lived in which house and that he should not be confused by the numbering as many of the former stables at the back had been converted into separate mews houses.

The exchange continued for some twenty minutes at the end of which Peter was asked:

—What do you do when not working for the Post Office? Are you perhaps an actor waiting for your next role? I can see that this is not your regular work.

—No, Sir, I have just completed my first term as an undergraduate.

—And may I enquire at which university?

—I am studying for my degree at Trinity College in Dublin.

—How interesting! I am the Chancellor of Trinity College!

An unexpected courtship

Archie Bannock-Kerr was the eldest son of a distinguished family. For several generations the family had produced senior military officers from the time of the Battle of Waterloo to the Second World War.

As the son of this distinguished family, he was born to inherited wealth and social prestige and was brought up with all its privileges. He was educated at Eton College from where he went to Sandhurst, the prestigious military academy, and was subsequently commissioned as a young lieutenant in the Coldstream Guards, the regiment to which three previous generations of his family had been members.

At the age of twenty two he was proud, and not a little arrogant, in keeping with his background as part of an elite class. His status as a young commissioned officer in a prestigious regiment gave him *entrée* to high society and he was much sought after by mothers seeking to find an eligible husband for their daughters.

With this inheritance, he could afford to dress expensively at Savile Row, dine at the best restaurants, own a sports car and generally live the high life. At the week-ends when he was off-duty he and his fellow officers liked to play polo and throw wild parties. His extrovert and confident style made him attractive to the opposite sex and he was never short of a glamorous and well-to-do companion. Life and all its benefits existed for his indulgence.

After two years of parties and social events, he decided one bored Sunday afternoon to pay a visit to a favourite aunt who lived on a country estate about thirty miles from the capital. There had always been a special bond between the two and during his childhood he had spent many happy times at her home where he was able to get away from the austerity of his parent's self-consciousness social position.

The aunt was a humorous and gentle soul who had once been a great beauty and a much sought-after debutante in the 1910 social season. She was now the mother of six, all born within a period of eight years. Although her house was full of servants she no longer had the time nor the inclination to socialize as she had done before. Her life was centred round the upbringing of her family and the activities of the local community;

nevertheless, she retained fond memories of the heady days as a young debutante and particularly enjoyed discussing these on the occasional visits from her nephew.

When still a debutante she had been courted by a number of eligible *beaux* from prestigious families but had fallen in love with the second son of an impoverished aristocratic who had known better times. Her husband was a vicar in the Protestant faith. However, in spite of his limited stipend, the family through his wife had the means to live in the style to which they had both been brought up.

Like most relationships in the world of high society, friendships are frequently superficial. In the case of Archie and his aunt, the friendship transcended the generation gap and was based on the love of entertaining, otherwise known as the "gay life". When together they frequently gossiped and giggled about the goings-on of the famous and infamous personalities of the social world.

Archie enjoyed showing off, especially to those on whom he could count not to rebuff his extrovert extravagance. The summer's afternoon that he decided to visit his aunt he dressed in full ceremonial uniform and travelled in open sports car to her country mansion. She was delighted at the surprise visit and greeted him warmly.

She was very proud and thrilled to see him in his ceremonial uniform. The sight of such elegance reminded her of the heady days when she went to hunt balls where there were always young officers looking distinguished and handsome in full regimental regalia.

Given that it was a beautiful summer's day, the aunt suggested that they sit on the veranda and enjoy the view across the lake. After a short interlude she called for tea and soon a maid arrived pushing a trolley laden with finely cut sandwiches and cakes. Once tea had been served from a Georgian silver service, they began the serious business of the latest gossip in fashionable circles. There was much laughter and merriment.

Two of the aunt's six children were still babies and were on the veranda nearby sleeping in prams. One of the babies suddenly awoke having been disturbed by an insect and began to cry. To show what a gentleman he was he jumped to his feet and approached the pram. He lifted the child and cradled it in his arms whereupon the startled baby, much to Archie's horror, burped over his uniform staining the braid. Horrified he sought to hand the child to its mother but she was in fits of laughter and refused to take the child until she had taken a photo of him holding his cousin.

He was mortified and, having suddenly realized that he had perhaps over done the gentlemanly act, he was feeling sheepish and embarrassed. To make amends, he made a supreme effort to turn the conversation to his aunt and her beautiful babies. She expressed polite gratitude at his interest but was not impressed although she did not want to hurt his feelings by letting on her real thoughts.

Like most of life, especially in the rarefied air of high society, things are said and done because they are "expected". For socialites, "good manners", frequently referred to as "good breeding", is a game the object of which is to maintain social status through, self promotion, exaggeration and self-importance. The young officer was still learning.

The attention that he had shown to the baby to impress his aunt was to have unexpected consequences. Little could he imagine that this same baby, his cousin, would be his wife twenty years later and that there was a photo recording their first encounter.

Good intentions

Brian Agnew was most foreigners' idea of the typical Englishman. He was tall and distinguished looking and always smartly dressed in a Savile Row suit with shoes highly polished and a carnation in his jacket button-hole.

He was educated at one of the finest private schools in England and studied for his degree at Oxford. At the age of twenty three he joined a prestigious merchant bank in the City of London at which he spent the whole of his working life ending his career as a director. He took himself very seriously, just as many people imagine a typical Englishman gentleman might do, and outwardly had all the characteristics associated with his background. He was formal, polite and confident but stiff in manner finding it difficult to communicate with the unfamiliar, in particular foreigners, children and pets. He was a man governed by his background and social standing.

He had lived all his adult life in the same house in a smart part of Central London. He was married to Sally, but rarely had time to spend at home. His wife had accepted this and had learnt to be independent, their few private moments being the occasional evening dinner together. Now that he was retired, Sally was reluctant to change her lifestyle to accommodate his new circumstances.

Since the children had grown up and had left home, Sally's time had been her own and her life for several years had revolved around her friends. She was used to spending time going out to lunch, shopping, visiting museums and going to matinee concerts and theatres.

Without work which had been his only interest and a wife who managed her own life, retirement was proving something of a shock. As he was no longer needed in a work situation, he had lost the sense of his own worth. For the first time in his life, there was self-doubt. This was not helped by the attitude of his wife who was resenting his continuing presence around the house and his constant querying as to what she was doing.

Brian was not interested in sports, had always had little time for leisure reading and had no abiding interests. His former business associates were not in regular contact, except for the occasional lunch, and, in the six months since his retirement, he had spent his time reading the newspapers, doing the "Times" crossword and following his stock market investments.

It was not in his make-up to be indolent and he realized that he had to do something. In addition, he had to get out of the house as he was aware of the irritation his constant presence was causing. He decided to let his position be known discreetly to a few trusted friends and they had come up at various times with the following ideas: that he accept a vacancy as Secretary of the Guild of Plumbers; that he volunteer to head the City Division of the Boys Brigade; that he become a hospital visitor, and even that he consider acting as a house-sitter. His sense of his own worth would not allow him to contemplate such proposals.

On refusing these offers, his wife got further irritated telling him that he was too proud for his own good. In the past, when annoyed by his wife's observations, he had had no difficulty asserting himself but now that his self-esteem was low, he felt further humiliated.

Several more months passed and no new opportunities occurred that he deemed worthy of his consideration. Eventually, however, he received a telephone call from a former banking associate inviting him to join the Board of Governors of a mental hospital in Bexley, a town not too far from London and therefore within easy travelling distance from his home. He thought about this offer and considered that as he would be a Director it could be a suitable position for someone of his social standing.

He was invited to lunch in the City to meet the other members of the Board, all of whom held prestigious positions in finance and business and, to his delight, discovered that he had been to school with one of them. This for him was reassuring that it would be a socially acceptable position and that he would be among his "own kind", a matter of importance.

After receiving official confirmation of his appointment, he was duly advised of the date of the next Board meeting. On the appointed day, he decided to familiarize himself with his new responsibilities by arriving in advance of the meeting. He drove in his car to Bexley and entered the grounds of the Home, parking his car outside the main entrance of the large purpose built Victorian building.

After introducing himself to the porter at the reception, he was given a guided tour of the premises by one of the care-takers. During the tour which included an explanation as to the different degrees of mental disorders and how they were dealt with, he was also briefed about the aims of the Home and how these had developed since the founding of the institution in 1899. He was also informed that many of the patients were in such a distressed state that some of them needed special restraining facilities to avoid them from harming themselves and giving stress to the other inmates. For a man who had spent his life in the sophisticated world of high finance, what he was learning was very chastening and he felt humbled by the misfortunes of others.

On completion of the tour of the premises which included all the communal areas and the special facilities, he was presented to the manager of the Home who took him to his office and, over a cup of tea, explained the problems and rewards of this type of work. Brian was impressed by the facilities and, in particular, the commitment of the staff.

After the briefing, he asked whether it would be in order to walk round the grounds and talk to some of the patients whom he had seen working outside on arrival. He was informed that this would be appreciated as the patients who were able to help maintain the grounds were the less mentally ill and did not present a risk. It was also explained that all contact with normal people helped them to socialize.

On leaving the manager's office, he walked out of the building into the gardens. It was a fine summer's day and he observed a working party weeding and pruning rose bushes under the supervision of a warden. He approached the warden explaining who he was and asked if he could be introduced to his charges. The guard readily agreed and accompanied him as he walked down the row of bushes and engaged the workers in conversation. He tried to be light-hearted but found it difficult to hold their attention. In reply to many of his well-intended enquiries, he was uncomfortable with the non coherent replies, accompanied, as often as not, by abuse or obscenities. He was disconcerted that he was unable to make real contact. Nevertheless, in line with his sense of commitment, he persevered down the row of bushes.

As he approached the end of the line, one of the workers jumped to his feet and shook his hand. They engaged in a normal conversation, much to Brian's surprise, and he wondered why this man was among the patients. As Brian was about to move on, the man asked him:-

—Excuse me, Sir, are you the new Governor?

—Yes, indeed I am and that is why I have wanted to meet you and your friends.

—Thank you, Sir. I have been here a number of years and I am now cured of my depression. I would very much like to be released and to return to a normal life.

Brian was surprised that a man who at some time in the past had, no doubt, been in a grave mental state, otherwise he would not be in the Home, could be so normal.

—Well —Brian replied— I can see that you are clearly in an improved state of mind but where would you go if you were released? Do you have family and do you think that you could find employment?

—Thank you, Sir, for recognizing my improved condition. And in answer to your questions, I have a sister who lives nearby who would be willing to take me in and, as for work, as a fully trained gardener, I am confident that I will be able to find employment.

—This is very encouraging —Brian replied— and I am pleased to have this opportunity to make a recommendation. I shall suggest your parole at this afternoon's Board of Governors' Meeting.

—Thank you, Sir, I have waited for this moment for a long while.

Much relieved that at least there had been one normal conversation, Brian bid farewell and continued to the end of the line. As he was about to return to the main building in time for the Board of Governors' Meeting, he received a heavy kick up his backside. It was so powerful that it knocked him over and he fell face down into a rose bush. The fall ruined his suit which had been torn by the thorns. His first thought was how on earth he was going to present himself to his new colleagues. He had never felt so foolish in his life and could not think how to explain what happened. As he gathered his thoughts and tried to regain his poise, he looked back and to his amazement saw the worker he had just been talking to waving a finger at him. Surprised and alarmed, he enquired of the fellow as he was being handcuffed and taken away by the warden:

—What prompted you to do that?

—Well, Sir, as a reminder of your promise and lest you forget!